Farmer's Market where Henry once ran away

Restaurant where kind man gives Henry and Eve ice cream

Apartment where Eve broke toilet

Pond where Henry dove in because he needed

to grab a fish

MONSTER'S LAIR

This book is for

Henry and Eve,

of course.

SIMON & SCHUSTER BOOKS FOR YOUNG READERS
An imprint of Simon & Schuster Children's Publishing Division
1230 Avenue of the Americas, New York, New York 10020
Copyright © 2010 by Lydecker Publishing, Inc.
All rights reserved, including the right of reproduction in whole or in part in any form.
SIMON & SCHUSTER BOOKS FOR YOUNG READERS is a trademark of Simon & Schuster, Inc.
For information about special discounts for bulk purchases, please contact Simon & Schuster Special Sales
at 1-866-506-1949 or business@simonandschuster.com.
The Simon & Schuster Speakers Bureau can bring authors to your live event. For more information or to book an event,
contact the Simon & Schuster Speakers Bureau at 1-866-248-3049 or visit our website at www.simonspeakers.com.
Book design by Lucy Ruth Cummins
The text for this book is set in Grit Primer.
The illustrations for this book are rendered in ink and watercolor.
Manufactured in China / 0112 SCP
6 8 10 9 7
Library of Congress Cataloging-in-Publication Data
Kaplan, Bruce Eric.
Monsters eat whiny children / Bruce Eric Kaplan. — 1st ed.
p. cm.
Summary: Henry and Eve, having ignored their father's warning,
are kidnapped by monsters who eat whiny children,
but while increasing numbers of monsters argue over how to prepare them,
the siblings begin to play nicely. Includes a recipe for cucumber sandwiches.
ISBN 978-1-4169-8689-8 (hardcover : alk. paper)
[1. Behavior—Fiction. 2. Monsters—Fiction. 3. Cookery—Fiction.
4. Brothers and sisters—Fiction] I. Title. PZ7.K128973Mon 2010
[E]—dc22
2008050434

MONSTERS EAT WHINY CHILDREN

BRUCE ERIC KAPLAN

SIMON & SCHUSTER BOOKS FOR YOUNG READERS
NEW YORK LONDON TORONTO SYDNEY

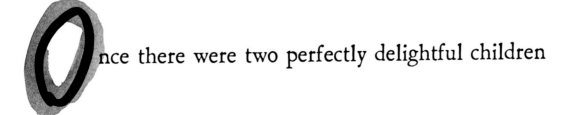

Once there were two perfectly delightful children

who were going through a TERRIBLE phase, which is to say they whined ALL day and night.

"I want to go outside," whined Henry.

"Outside! Outside!" whined Eve.

"Where's my phone?" whined Henry.

"No grilled cheese!" whined Eve.

And so on.

Their kindly father warned them that monsters eat whiny children.

They didn't believe him. So they whined and whined until finally one day

a monster came and stole them away.

He brought them back to his lair

on the bad side of town.

He began making a whiny-child salad.

"I don't like sitting on lettuce," Henry whined.

"No wooden bowl," whined Eve.

The monster made dressing, poured it on Henry and Eve, and called his wife in for dinner.

She sampled the dressing and spat it out.

"I hate cilantro!" she screamed.

"Start again, and this time use paprika."

"I hate paprika," said the monster.

"No, you don't," said his wife.

"Okay," he sighed.

So he hosed off Henry and Eve and made a new
dressing with paprika.

His wife tasted it.

"I love it," she said.

Everything was perfect.

But just as Henry and Eve were about to get back into
the wooden bowl, a neighbor dropped by and asked the
monsters what they were doing.

When they told him, the neighbor totally freaked out.

"You've got two wonderfully whiny children and you're going to make a stupid salad?" he said.

"All week long all I've wanted were

whiny-child burgers!

Let's grill these kids up now! Yum!"

The monster and his wife thought for a moment.

The neighbor said, **"C'mon! I can't wait another second.** I think I even dreamed about whiny-child burgers last night."

"Okay," said the monster.

His wife sighed because this meant she had to clean their grill, which was disgusting.

So they got the grill out from the back of the garage, cleaned it, and tried to make a good fire. But the monster couldn't do it, nor his wife, nor his neighbor, because it's hard to get a fire going sometimes.

Henry started to whine but then got distracted by a ball.

He rolled it over to Eve while the monsters were cursing at the grill.

Finally they asked the neighbor's cousin to come over since he was good with grills.

But he couldn't start a fire either.

So he kicked a hole in the fence

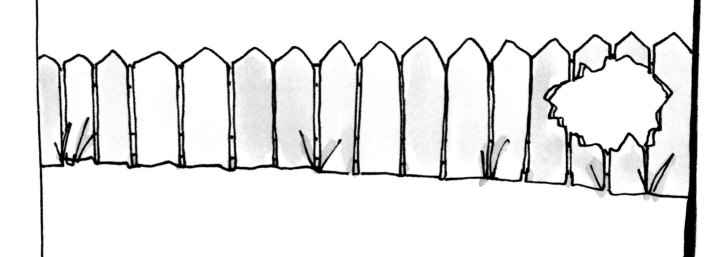

and said, "You should make a whiny-child cake anyway."

The monster's wife said she couldn't eat sweets because her bottom was too big.

Everyone told her she was crazy.

"Besides, I hate baking," she said.

"I'll do it," said the neighbor's cousin.

He started to assemble the ingredients to make the cake, but there was a terrible accident

and all the flour spilled all over the floor.

So now they couldn't make the cake. Plus, the oven had been preheating, so the kitchen was hot and everyone was sweaty.

"Why does everything have to be so hard?" asked the monster.

"Anything worth doing involves a struggle," offered the neighbor.

Henry felt bad for the monster, so
he rolled the ball over to him. The
monster bounced it against the wall
and felt a little better.

Eve looked around for something else to play with.
She found some cars in the corner. She pushed one over
to Henry, who happily made it crash into another car.

"We could make some rice, put a
little curry on them, and have an Indian
dish," someone suggested halfheartedly.

"Perhaps a whiny-child vindaloo."

They all tried to figure out if they were in the mood for
Indian food.

Sometimes it's so hard to figure out if you're in the
mood for Indian food.

As the monster's wife looked for some trucks to give to Henry and Eve, she thought about the last time she ate Indian food. It hadn't agreed with her and she wondered if that would happen again.

"No Indian food!" she decided.

"What's going on here?" someone yelled in a loud nasal voice.

Everyone turned around to find the monster's aunt entering, angry at the world as she always was.

They told her about their day and she yelled at them.

"For Pete's sake,"

she said, hitting the

neighbor's cousin with some

spittle because she had a

saliva problem.

"You should just make

a simple whiny-child

cucumber sandwich."

"Yes! Yes! Yes! Yes! Yes!" they all said, and jumped up and down.

It's such a relief to finally figure out what the right thing to eat is.

"Enough of this nonsense," said the monster's aunt.

"Let's start making the sandwiches."

The monster excitedly went to the cupboard and found a nice loaf of healthy twelve-grain bread.

"For Pete's sake," his aunt spat, "everyone knows you need fluffy white bread!"

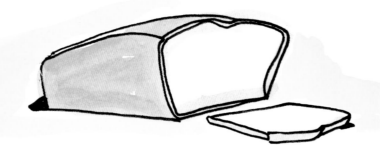

The monster explained that he hadn't eaten white bread in years, but the neighbor quickly ran next door and came back with the fluffiest white bread anyone had ever seen.

Next they had to add the whiny children, but they turned around to find that

Henry and Eve had
somehow escaped.

So they all sat down and ate the cucumber sandwiches which, while not like ones with whiny children, were absolutely delicious anyway.

And here is the recipe:

CUCUMBER SANDWICHES

1. Lay out slices of fluffy white bread.

2. Spread mayonnaise (or cream cheese or butter) all over them.

3. Slice some cucumbers and put on some of the bread.

4. Put the rest of the bread on top and they are all ready to SERVE!

Meanwhile, Henry and Eve ran back home and never whined again.

Although to tell you the truth,

every now and then they did.

HENRY AND EVE'S HOUSE

Place where Henry and Eve lost their little stroller

Neighbors' where Henry totally freaked out one Halloween

Store where people think Eve is a boy

Park where Henry and Eve go every day almost

Library where Henry and Eve like to be too loud